A Beginning-to-Read Book

Dear Dragon Flies a Kite

by Margaret Hillert

Illustrated by Jack Pullan

NORWOOD HOUSE PRESS

DEAR CAREGIVER, The *Beginning-to-Read* series is a carefully written collection of classic readers you may remember from your own childhood. Each book features text comprised of common sight words to provide your child ample practice reading the words that appear most frequently in written text. The many additional details in the pictures enhance the story and offer the opportunity for you to help your child expand oral language and develop comprehension.

Begin by reading the story to your child, followed by letting him or her read familiar words and soon your child will be able to read the story independently. At each step of the way, be sure to praise your reader's efforts to build his or her confidence as an independent reader. Discuss the pictures and encourage your child to make connections between the story and his or her own life. At the end of the story, you will find reading activities and a word list that will help your child practice and strengthen beginning reading skills.

Above all, the most important part of the reading experience is to have fun and enjoy it!

Shannon Cannon

Shannon Cannon, Ph.D.
Literacy Consultant

Norwood House Press • P.O. Box 316598 • Chicago, Illinois 60631
For more information about Norwood House Press please visit our website at
www.norwoodhousepress.com or call 866-565-2900.

Text copyright ©2015 by Margaret Hillert. Illustrations and cover design copyright ©2015 by Norwood House Press, Inc. All rights reserved. No part of this book may be reproduced or utilized in any form or by any means without written permission from the publisher.

LIBRARY OF CONGRESS CATALOGING-IN-PUBLICATION DATA
   Hillert, Margaret.
      Dear Dragon flies a kite / by Margaret Hillert ; illustrated by Jack Pullan.
         pages cm. -- (A Beginning-to-read book)
      Summary: "A boy and his pet dragon learn how to fly a kite. When dragon takes flight with the kite he is able to explore their neighborhood and surrounding areas. This title includes reading activities and a word list"-- Provided by publisher.
      ISBN 978-1-59953-674-3 (library edition : alk. paper) -- ISBN 978-1-60357-734-2 (ebook)
      [1. Kites--Fiction. 2. Dragons--Fiction.] I. Pullan, Jack, illustrator. II. Title.
      PZ7.H558Ddp 2015
      [E]--dc23
                                          2014030276

262N—122014
Manufactured in the United States of America in North Mankato, Minnesota.

What is that?
What do you have there?
What is that red and orange thing?
Is it something to play with?

Oh, yes.
It is something to play with,
but it needs wind to make it go.

I will show you.

Run, run, run, and
help it go up.

It is going up!
It is going up!

Oh, oh.
Dragon is going up too!
You are way, way up Dear Dragon.
Look down, look down.
What do you see down here?

Can you see the house?
Can you see Mother and Sister?

Can you see our school?
Do you see the blue car?

Do you see the farm?
Do you see the horse?

Do you see the river?
Do you see a boat in the river?

Do you see the nest in the tree?
Do you see baby birds in the nest?

Look out!
Look out!
Look out for the tree!

Oh, oh.
Now you are in the tree.

We can get Dear Dragon down.

Dear Dragon is alright.
But the kite is not good.
We will get a new kite.

Yes, we will need a new kite.

Oh, Dear Dragon.
It is good to have you down.

Here you are with me.
And here I am with you.
Oh what a good day, Dear Dragon.

READING REINFORCEMENT

The following activities support the findings of the National Reading Panel that determined the most effective components for reading instruction are: Phonemic Awareness, Phonics, Vocabulary, Fluency, and Text Comprehension.

Phonemic Awareness: The /k/ sound

Oddity Task: Say the /**k**/ sound for your child. Ask your child to say the word that has the /**k**/ sound in the following word groups:

kid, rid, bid	rock, run, road	pan, pat, pack
back, barn, band	sock, saw, sat	find, kind, mind

Phonics: The letter Kk

1. Demonstrate how to form the letters **K** and **k** for your child.

2. Have your child practice writing **K** and **k** at least three times each.

3. Write down the following words and ask your child to circle the letter **k** in each word.

back	dark	make	king	book
look	work	like	lock	duck
kite	truck	key	milk	kid

Vocabulary: Nouns and Verbs

1. Write the following words on separate pieces of paper and point to them as you read them to your child:

go	mother	house	jump	father
boy	work	run	girl	tree

2. Point to each word and read it aloud to your child. Ask your child to repeat the word.

3. Explain to your child that words describing people, places, and things are called nouns, and that words describing actions are called verbs.

4. Divide a piece of paper in half vertically and write the words nouns and verbs at the top, one in each column.

5. Ask your child to sort the words on the pieces of paper by placing them in the correct column depending on whether the word on the paper is a noun or a verb.

6. Continue identifying nouns and verbs by playing a game in which one of you names a noun and the other names a verb to go with the noun. (For example: dog/bark, baby/cry, grass/grow, flower/bloom, car/drive, etc.)

Fluency: Echo Reading

1. Reread the story to your child at least two more times while your child tracks the print by running a finger under the words as they are read. Ask your child to read the words he or she knows with you.

2. Reread the story, stopping after each sentence or page to allow your child to read (echo) what you have read. Repeat echo reading and let your child take the lead.

Text Comprehension: Discussion Time

1. Ask your child to retell the sequence of events in the story.

2. To check comprehension, ask your child the following questions:

   • How do Dear Dragon and the boy make the kite go?

   • What are some things Dear Dragon saw when he was in the sky?

   • What happened to Dear Dragon on page 23?

   • Have you ever been up in the sky? What did you see? If you have not been in the sky, what do you think you would see?

WORD LIST

Dear Dragon Flies a Kite **uses the 71 words listed below.**

The **7** words bolded below serve as an introduction to new vocabulary, while the other 64 are pre-primer. You may wish to write the words on index cards and use them to help your child build automatic word recognition. Regular practice with these words will enhance your child's fluency in reading connected text.

a	farm	kite	red	way
alright	for		**river**	we
am		look	run	what
and	get			will
are	go	make	school	**wind**
	going	me	see	with
baby	good	Mother	**show**	
birds			**Sister**	yes
blue	have	need(s)	something	you
boat	help	**nest**		
but	here	**new**	that(s)	
	horse	not	the	
can	house	now	there	
car			thing	
	I	oh	to	
day	in	orange	too	
Dear	is	our	tree	
do	it	out		
down			up	
Dragon		play		

ABOUT THE AUTHOR   Margaret Hillert has written over 80 books for children who are just learning to read. Her books have been translated into many different languages and over a million children throughout the world have read her books. She first started writing poetry as a child and has continued to write for children and adults throughout her life. A first grade teacher for 34 years, Margaret is now retired from teaching and lives in Michigan where she likes to write, take walks in the morning, and care for her three cats.

Photograph by Glenna Washburn

ABOUT THE ILLUSTRATOR   A talented and creative illustrator, Jack Pullan, is a graduate of William Jewell College. He has also studied informally at Oxford University and the Kansas City Art Institute. He was mentored by the renowned watercolor artists, Jim Hamil and Bill Amend. Jack's work has graced the pages of many enjoyable children's books, various educational materials, cartoon strips, as well as many greeting cards. Jack currently resides in Kansas.